# Pirates of Bikini Bottom

Pirates of Bikini Bottom

by David Lewman

illustrated by Harry Moore

SCHOLASTIC INC.

New York  Toronto  London  Auckland  Sydney
Mexico City  New Delhi  Hong Kong  Buenos Aires

*Stephen Hillenburg*

Based on the TV series *SpongeBob SquarePants*®
created by Stephen Hillenburg as seen on Nickelodeon®

ISBN-13: 978-0-545-00813-6
ISBN-10: 0-545-00813-1

12 11 10 9 8 7 6 5 4 3 2 1          7 8 9 10 11 12/0

Printed in the U.S.A.

First Scholastic printing, November 2007

Look for these other
# SpongeBob SquarePants
chapter books!

# chapter one

At the Krusty Krab, SpongeBob was on his lunch break. He sat with Patrick, each of them enjoying a delicious Krabby Patty. "Go ahead, Patrick," he told his best friend confidently. "Ask me another one."

Patrick stopped chewing for a moment and thought hard. "Okay, um . . . um . . . oh, I know!" he said, excited to have thought of a question. "How many sesame seeds are on top of a Krabby Patty bun?"

SpongeBob smiled. "That's easy, Patrick. There are exactly four hundred twenty-eight sesame seeds baked into a wholesome Krabby Patty bun. What else you got?"

Patrick frowned. "Hmm . . . how many Krabby Patties does the Krusty Krab serve on Tuesdays?"

SpongeBob leaned back and put his hands behind his head. "Summer Tuesdays or winter Tuesdays?"

"Um . . . summer," answered Patrick with his mouth full.

Grinning, SpongeBob said, "Excellent question. On an average Tuesday in summer, the Krusty Krab serves one thousand two hundred fifty-six Krabby Patties."

"Boy, you're good," said Patrick as he finished his sandwich. Then he looked up from the empty wrapper. "You too, SpongeBob."

"Ask another, Patrick!" SpongeBob was enjoying showing off his detailed knowledge of Krabby Patties. As the number one fry cook in Bikini Bottom, he prided himself on knowing everything there was to know about the town's yummiest sandwich.

Patrick stopped licking the wrapper of his sandwich. He wrinkled his forehead, searching his brain for another question. "Well . . . um . . . um . . . oh, okay! Here's one! Why is the Krabby Patty called a Krabby Patty?"

"Simple!" exclaimed SpongeBob. "Because, uh, because, uh . . ." SpongeBob was stunned. He didn't know the answer!

"I'll be right back!" he cried as he jumped to his feet and raced to Mr.

Krabs's office. SpongeBob pounded on the door marked CAPTAIN.

"Mr. Krabs! Mr. Krabs!" he shouted. From behind the door he heard his boss grumble, "Come in, SpongeBob."

SpongeBob burst into Mr. Krabs's office. "Mr. Krabs! I have a question about Krabby Patties!"

Mr. Krabs sighed. "Right now, me lad, I'm not very interested in Krabby Patties."

SpongeBob staggered against a chair, shocked to his very core. How could anyone, let alone the owner of the Krusty Krab, not care about Krabby Patties? "Mr. Krabs," whispered SpongeBob, "what's wrong?"

Mr. Krabs got up from his chair and stared out the window, a faraway look in his eyes. "To tell you the truth, SpongeBob, I'm a little tired of the restaurant business. I miss the days when

I was sailing the six seas."

SpongeBob looked puzzled. "Don't you mean the *seven* seas, Mr. Krabs?"

"Back then, there were only six," Mr. Krabs growled. Then he smiled wistfully. "Ah, that was the life! Living on a ship, seeing new places, meeting new people, and never having to listen to Squidward complain!"

"Gee, Mr. Krabs, I wish there was something I could do to cheer you up," offered Sponge-Bob. Mr. Krabs patted him on the head.

"There's nothing you can do, boy," he said, "except get back to work!"

"Aye, aye, Captain, sir," SpongeBob said as he quickly returned to the dining room, where Patrick had just polished off SpongeBob's Krabby Patty. "I, uh, didn't think you were coming back," he said, wiping his mouth.

But SpongeBob didn't care about his sandwich. He had something much more important on his mind. "Listen, Patrick," he said. "We've got to think of a way to cheer up Mr. Krabs!"

"Ooh, ooh, I know! How about building a house of cards?" Patrick said eagerly.

SpongeBob shook his head. "That idea's not big enough."

"Two houses of cards?" suggested Patrick.

SpongeBob snapped his fingers. "I've got it!" he yelled. "The perfect idea for cheering up Mr. Krabs! But I'm going to need your help, buddy."

"Way ahead of you, pal," replied Patrick, holding up a deck of cards.

# chapter two

That night while the rest of Bikini Bottom was sound asleep, SpongeBob and Patrick tiptoed to the Krusty Krab. They carried plenty of wood, paint, canvas, and tools.

"Explain this to me again," whispered Patrick, his arms full of boards and rope.

"It's simple," answered SpongeBob. "Mr. Krabs misses working on a ship, right?"

"I don't know," Patrick replied. He dropped the materials on the ground.

"Well, he does," said SpongeBob. "So we're going to make the whole Krusty Krab restaurant look like a big ship!"

Patrick stared up at the outside of the building. "What does it look like now?"

"I don't know. Kind of like a lobster trap, I guess," replied SpongeBob, shrugging.

"Hmm . . . maybe that's why Larry the Lobster never eats here," Patrick said.

The two friends got right to work, sawing and hammering as quietly as they could. At first Patrick hit his hand almost as often as he hit the nails, but eventually he got better at it. They were making pretty good progress when a Bikini Bottom policeman strolled up.

"All right," he said, "what do you think you're doing?"

"Answering your question," said Patrick honestly.

The policeman looked annoyed. "I mean, what were you doing before I asked you that question?"

"Wondering what you were going to ask us," said SpongeBob.

The policeman exploded with anger. "I MEAN, WHAT DO YOU THINK YOU'RE DOING HAMMERING AWAY AT THE KRUSTY KRAB IN THE MIDDLE OF THE NIGHT?"

SpongeBob set down his hammer. "Oh!" he said. "Well, you see, Mr. Krabs is depressed."

"So?" grunted the policeman.

"And if he's depressed, he can't do a good job of running the Krusty Krab," explained SpongeBob.

"So?" repeated the policeman.

"And if the Krusty Krab isn't run well, it might go out of business," SpongeBob continued.

"Yeah?" The policeman sneered.

"And then there wouldn't be any more Krabby Patties," SpongeBob said.

The policeman suddenly looked very worried. "What? No more delicious, mouthwatering Krabby Patties?"

Patrick nodded. "That's right, officer."

"Carry on, then," said the policeman. "Whatever it takes to cheer Krabs up, just do it!" He quickly walked away, leaving Sponge-

Bob and Patrick to continue their project.

It took all night, but by morning the restaurant actually looked quite a bit like a big ship, complete with prow, mast, sail, deck, steering wheel, and rudder. Tired but happy, SpongeBob and Patrick stood back and admired their work.

"What is *that*?"

Squidward had arrived for work, and he was very surprised to see what SpongeBob and Patrick had done.

SpongeBob beamed with pride. "It's a new look for the Krusty Krab, Squidward! What do you think?"

Squidward just shook his head. "I think you two dunderheads are in big trouble."

"Trouble?" asked SpongeBob. "What kind of trouble could we get into by making the Krusty Krab look like a ship?"

"AHOY THERE, YE SCURVY DOGS! PRE-PARE TO BE BOARDED!"

They all turned around and saw a band of pirates running straight toward the Krusty Krab!

"Uh, this kind of trouble," Squidward muttered.

# chapter three

"Ahhhhhhhhh!" screamed Squidward. But that didn't slow down the pirates one bit. They came barreling toward the Krusty Krab at top speed. Three of the biggest and ugliest pirates grabbed SpongeBob, Patrick, and Squidward and pulled them all to the roof of the Krusty Krab.

"This'll make a fine pirate ship!" cried a tall pirate with fierce eyes and a long black beard filled with bits of food. "Raise the flag!"

Faster than anyone could say "Jolly Roger," the pirates attached a black flag with a skull and crossbones to the mast. When it reached the top of the pole, they all cheered!

"Um, excuse me, Mr. Pirate, sir," stammered SpongeBob meekly. "But this isn't really a ship. It's a restaurant."

The tall pirate whirled around and stared at SpongeBob. "Ahrrr, I say it's a pirate ship, or me name's not Crumbeard! And since we lost our ship, it's just what we need!"

Squidward stepped forward. He had gotten over his initial fright and was now his usual annoyed self. "Listen, buddy, we need to speak to your captain."

Crumbeard's expression immediately changed. "We don't have a captain," he said sadly. "We lost him, too." All the pirates hung their heads for a moment, then went back to swarming all over the Krusty Krab.

"Anyway, we're taking this ship," said Crumbeard. He glared at Squidward, SpongeBob, and Patrick. From the look on his face, it was clear he wasn't interested in hearing any arguments. "And our crew is short three pirates, so we're taking you three landlubbers with us!"

"Us? Pirates?" asked Patrick.

"Take us where?" shouted Squidward. "In case you haven't noticed, this is a cheap fast-food restaurant, and like my career, it isn't going anywhere!"

Turning to the other pirates, Crumbeard shouted, "Pull up the anchor!" They started pulling on a huge chain, and soon a huge, heavy anchor hung off the back of the building.

"Hoist the mainsail!" cried another pirate, and a full, white sail waved from the mast. Suddenly the Krusty Krab began to move!

The whole building lurched forward. "What's happening?" Squidward yelled as he fell to the deck.

"We're settin' sail!" called Crumbeard happily.

SpongeBob watched as the restaurant slid away from the Krusty Krab sign. He spotted a small figure walking toward the spot where the restaurant normally stood. "Mr. Krabs!" he cried. "Help!"

Mr. Krabs looked up and saw that his restaurant was sailing away. "Stop! Wait! That's my Krusty Krab! Come back!"

Huffing and puffing, Mr. Krabs ran after the Krusty Krab, but it was too late. The wooden building sailed out of town and over the horizon with SpongeBob, Patrick, and Squidward onboard.

# chapter four

SpongeBob stood at the railing as his beloved Bikini Bottom disappeared from sight. A tear dripped off his nose. "This is terrible!" he cried. "Where will people go for Krabby Patties?"

Crumbeard strode up and slapped SpongeBob on the back. "Cheer up, little sponge!" he said, laughing. "You're a pirate now! And pirates don't cry!"

"They don't?" asked SpongeBob, wiping

away a tear. He sniffed sadly.

"Well, hardly ever," admitted Crumbeard. "You know what new pirates do?"

"No. What?" SpongeBob asked.

Crumbeard handed SpongeBob a mop. "They swab the deck, me hearty!" the tall pirate shouted with laughter. Then he walked away, leaving SpongeBob with the mop.

Well, at least I know how to do this, thought SpongeBob as he started cleaning the roof of the Krusty Krab. I do it every day!

Rotty, a pirate with a wooden leg, told Patrick to climb up to the crow's nest and be the lookout. But as soon as he said "lookout," Patrick whirled around, scared. "What? Where?" he cried. The rest of the crew laughed.

Rotty frowned. "I said, climb up and be the lookout!"

"What? Where?" Patrick asked again as he whirled around. The pirates laughed even louder. Then Rotty got a sly look on his face.

"Lookout!"

"What? Where?"

"Lookout!"

"What? Where?"

"Lookout!"

"What? Where?"

Each time Patrick whirled around trying to see what he should "lookout" for, the pirates laughed harder, until all three of them were rolling on the deck of the ship clutching their sides and slapping their thighs—and Patrick was dizzy and about to fall down from all that spinning. Finally Rotty hauled Patrick over to the mast and pushed him up into the crow's nest.

Meanwhile, a big pirate named Tarnish, with a hook for a hand, looked Squidward up and down, trying to decide what he could possibly be good at doing.

"Ahrrr, let me see," said Tarnish. "Ye have two arms, four legs—"

"Yeah, so what?" Squidward interrupted.

"And a big mouth," the pirate said, scowling. "Get to work smoothin' these wooden legs." He pointed to a big pile of wooden pegs, stained and rough with plenty of long, sharp splinters.

"No, thank you!" barked Squidward, turning

his back on the pirate. The pirate scratched his head with his hook, not sure what to do.

SpongeBob had finished mopping the roof, so he stood before Crumbeard saluting. "The deck is all swabbed, sir!" The pirate looked at the floor. It was so clean he could see himself reflected in it!

"Smartly done, sponge!" Crumbeard said, nodding approvingly.

"What would you like me to do next, sir?" asked SpongeBob.

The big pirate shrugged. "I don't know. I'm so hungry, I can't think straight."

"You're hungry? I know just what to do," SpongeBob said, and ran down to the kitchen.

When he brought up a batch of delicious, mouthwatering Krabby Patties, the pirates crowded around. Within seconds all the Krabby Patties were gone, and the pirates called for more. SpongeBob kept them coming as fast as the pirates could eat them!

"Can I have a Krabby Patty?" called Patrick from high up in the crow's nest.

"But Patrick, you have to keep looking out for . . . whatever it is you're looking out for!" SpongeBob replied.

"No problem!" shouted Patrick. He put his arms around the mast, slid down to the deck,

grabbed a Krabby Patty, ate it in one bite, and slid back up the pole to the crow's nest. The pirates all laughed. They had never seen anyone do that before!

Then one of the pirates started dancing a sailor's jig called a hornpipe. When Sponge-Bob saw him, he played a tune on his nose that matched the pirate's dance perfectly. When he finished, the pirates cheered!

"Huzzah for the sponge!" called Crumbeard. "What can he not do, eh? He can swab, cook, and play better than any pirate I've ever seen!"

"And huzzah for the starfish!" shouted Rotty. "He makes us laugh!"

"What about this one?" asked Tarnish, holding Squidward up by the scruff of his neck.

"What about him?" asked Rotty, sneering at Squidward.

"He refuses to work!" Tarnish said. He spat on the ground. SpongeBob ran over and quickly wiped up the spit.

The pirates all stared at Squidward angrily. "Then he'll have to be punished," growled Crumbeard.

# chapter five

"Punished?" squeaked SpongeBob. "Uh, how would he be punished?"

Rotty smiled, showing a mouth full of ugly rotten teeth. "Ahrrr, there be all kinds of great pirate punishments—like walking the plank, keelhauling . . ."

Squidward looked nervous. "How about if you just confine me to my quarters with a good book and a jar of fancy olives?" He flashed a smile, trying to change the pirates' minds.

"It's not up to you!" roared Tarnish. "That's for the captain to decide!"

"But you said you don't have a captain," SpongeBob said. The pirates nodded and shuffled their feet, unsure what to do. Then Crumbeard had an idea.

"Fellow pirates!" he called to everyone onboard. "'Tis time we elected a new captain!"

The pirates cheered in agreement. "A new captain!"

"Do I get to vote?" asked Squidward hopefully.

"No!" barked Rotty.

The pirates quickly organized the election. They used Krusty Krab napkins for the ballots and marked them with the pencils Squidward used to write down customers' orders. Once they had voted for a captain, they slipped their ballots into an empty pickle jar. Then they all counted the votes together.

When they were done, Crumbeard looked up from the pile of ballots. "Our new captain is . . . SpongeBob!"

SpongeBob couldn't believe it. He had never been a pirate before, let alone the captain of a pirate ship! His new crew cheered and lifted SpongeBob onto their shoulders.

"Wow! I guess pirates really like clean floors, delicious Krabby Patties, and nose music!" SpongeBob said.

The pirates found a big black hat and stuck it on SpongeBob's head. After draping a long coat around his shoulders, they set him on the quarterdeck, where he could address his crew.

Tarnish waved his hook toward SpongeBob. "Captain SpongeBob!" he shouted. "What do ye have to say to your faithful pirate crew?" All the pirates waited for him to speak.

SpongeBob looked at everyone and coughed into his hand. "Ahrrr," he finally said. "I think you can all agree with me when I simply say, 'Ahrrr.'"

The pirates politely murmured "Ahrrr" in return, but they weren't sure what Sponge-Bob was trying to say. SpongeBob continued, pacing back and forth as he spoke.

"For that is what pirates say, isn't it? Pirates say 'Ahrrr,' and so as your new captain, I join you in saying 'Ahrrr.' I think you will find that as your pirate captain, I will be tough but fair. I will divide booty evenly, and—"

"What about the punishment?" Rotty interrupted.

"Punishment? What punishment?" asked SpongeBob, confused. In the excitement of being elected captain, he'd forgotten all about having to pick a punishment for Squidward.

"For the lazy one!" answered Tarnish. "The one who refuses to work!"

"Oh, right," SpongeBob said, remembering. He looked around nervously. "Wouldn't you rather talk about treasure?"

"NO!" roared the pirates. "Punishment! Punishment! Punishment!" they chanted, pumping their fists and hooks in the air.

SpongeBob didn't know what to do. He didn't want Squidward to be punished. After all, the pirates had kidnapped him against his will. But if he didn't come up with a punishment for Squidward, what would the pirates do?

Just then a voice called out, "Uh, ahoy mateys, uh, SHIP HO!"

Everyone looked up. In the crow's nest, high above the deck, Patrick was pointing toward the horizon. All the pirates rushed to the side of the ship. Sure enough, they could see a large ship with purple sails in the distance. And it was heading straight toward them!

# chapter six

"Battle stations!" yelled SpongeBob. He wasn't sure what battle stations were, but it seemed like the right thing to say. The pirates ran and took their places all over the Krusty Krab as it waited to meet the new ship.

"Whew, at least I don't have to think about that for a while," SpongeBob muttered, relieved that the pirates were distracted from punishing Squidward.

Rotty pulled out a spyglass and peered

toward the ship. "Their flag carries a picture of an evil-looking creature with two antennae and one large eye."

That sounded familiar to SpongeBob. Who did he know with two antennae and one eye?

Suddenly a deep voice came through the mist. "Surrender!" it called. "Hand over your ship and all its recipes to me, for I am Captain Plankton!"

"Plankton!" said SpongeBob, surprised. "We can't let him take our ship! It's full of Krabby Patties! He'll be able to figure out the recipe!"

Squidward was standing beside SpongeBob, watching Plankton's ship get closer and closer. "What difference does that make?" he asked. "There is no Krusty Krab restaurant anymore! It's some kind of crazy boat now!"

SpongeBob turned to Squidward, his eyes full of steely determination. "Matey Squidward," he said. "As long as I'm captain of this ship, we are not going to let Plankton get his hands on a single Krabby Patty, with or without cheese!"

"Oh, brother," said Squidward as he slipped off to find a safe place to hide.

Plankton's ship had come so close that the two ships were practically touching. Plankton stood on the railing, leaning forward eagerly. "Give me your ship," he demanded, cupping his hands around his mouth, "or I'll send it to Davy Jones's locker!"

Patrick chuckled. "How are you going to fit a whole ship in a locker?"

SpongeBob climbed up onto the rail. "How are you going to take over this ship? You don't have a crew!" he challenged.

Plankton grinned. "Oh yes, I do!" he said, laughing maniacally. He pressed a button on a remote control, and dozens of robot pirates rolled up to the side of the boat!

The pirates on the Krusty Krab gasped and stepped back. They had never seen pirates like these before: built out of gleaming metal, with wheels for feet and a single glowing green eye in the middle of each forehead!

SpongeBob could tell the pirates were frightened by Plankton's menacing robot crew. "Don't be afraid!" he called.

"Why not?" asked Crumbeard.

SpongeBob couldn't come up with an answer right away. "Well . . . ," he began. But then he noticed Squidward climbing onto Plankton's ship, carrying a jar with a rolled-up piece of paper in it. It was the Krabby Patty recipe!

"Hey, Plankton," said Squidward casually.

"Look what I found while I was searching for a good hiding place—the secret formula!"

Plankton's eye bugged out, and he drooled a little. "Could it be? Could it actually be, after all these years?" He reached toward the jar, and Squidward stretched his tentacle to hand it to him.

"NOOOOO!" cried SpongeBob as he dove onto the deck of Plankton's ship, his hands reaching for the jar. The second his nose hit the floorboards, the robot pirates started zooming toward him. He tried to grab the recipe jar, but instead he knocked the remote control out of Plankton's hand. It fell to the ground and shattered into a hundred pieces!

The robots instantly slumped over—completely immobile. Plankton was horrified. "My crew! My beautiful pirate crew!" he groaned.

SpongeBob saw his chance. He grabbed

the jar, shoved Squidward back onto the Krusty
Krab, and leaped over the rail himself. "Push
the ship away!" he yelled to his pirate crew.

"Yeah, push!" called Patrick from the crow's nest.

Using whatever sticks or wooden legs they could find, the pirates shoved the ship away from the Krusty Krab. Now Plankton was helpless. He didn't have his remote control or his robot crew, and he couldn't sail the ship by himself. So he drifted away, calling, "Just you wait, SpongeBob!" and shaking his tiny fist.

When they saw that they were safe, the

pirates hoisted SpongeBob onto their shoulders and cheered, "Three huzzahs for Captain SpongeBob!"

Rotty clapped SpongeBob on the back. "That was fine pirate work, that was," he said admiringly. "Where would you like to sail to next, Captain? The Tiki Triangle? Amberjack Isle? Somewhere in search of treasure?"

SpongeBob grinned. It was fun being the captain of a pirate ship, and he loved the idea of finding treasure. But he knew where he really wanted to go. "I want to go home," Sponge-Bob said wistfully. "Back to Bikini Bottom."

A loud murmur filled the deck of the pirate ship as the crew heard SpongeBob's response. Tarnish held up his hand for silence before nodding and telling SpongeBob he understood.

Then he turned to the other pirates. "All right, boys!" he shouted. "Tie 'em up!"

# chapter seven

SpongeBob, Patrick, and Squidward sat back-to-back, tied tightly together with thick, sturdy rope. "Real smart, SpongeBob," said Squidward sarcastically. "You just had to tell these stupid pirates you wanted to go home."

"But I do want to go home," SpongeBob replied. "How was I supposed to know that meant I couldn't be captain anymore?"

Patrick squirmed, trying to get loose, but it was no use: When it comes to tying knots, pirates are the experts. "Squidward, weren't you're the one who tried to give away the Krabby Patty recipe?" he asked.

"Patrick, if you hadn't pointed out Plankton's ship in the first place . . ."

"QUIET!" shouted Crumbeard, leaning down over the three prisoners. "With all your bickering, we can't even hear ourselves think!"

"What are you trying to think of?" asked SpongeBob.

"A really good way to punish you." Rotty smirked. "And from what I hear, walking the plank is definitely in the lead."

"Do you pirates spend all your time voting and punishing?" muttered Squidward.

"I SAID, QUIET!" Crumbeard bellowed.

With Patrick tied up, Tarnish had taken his place up in the crow's nest. Suddenly his golden hook flashed in the sun as he pointed to something in the distance. "SHIP AHOY!" he cried.

"Maybe Plankton fixed his remote control," SpongeBob whispered hopefully. But the ship that was rapidly sailing toward the Krusty Krab wasn't Plankton's. It was a yellow ship with red trim, and a big red claw on its flag. And standing proudly at the bow of the ship, a grim look on his face, was Mr. Krabs!

He sailed expertly right up alongside the Krusty Krab and jumped over the rail. Wasting no time, he walked straight up to Crumbeard, looked him in the eye, and said, "Ahrrr. I want me restaurant back. It's how I make me money."

The pirates were silent for a moment. Then they started to laugh. "So you're going to steal our ship, old man?" jeered Rotty.

"No," said Mr. Krabs, shaking his head. "I'm going to trade you. Give me back the Krusty Krab, and you can have the ship I used to find you."

Tarnish came down from the crow's nest and pointed his hook at Mr. Krabs. "I've got a better idea!" he said. "We'll keep the Krusty Krab *and* take the new ship too!"

The pirates roared their approval. But Mr. Krabs just stood there, shaking his head. "I'm afraid that's not possible," he said. "You see, my secret weapon wouldn't like it."

"Secret weapon?" said Crumbeard. "What secret weapon?"

Mr. Krabs put his face very close to the big pirate's. "A land squirrel," he said in a low, even voice.

Crumbeard guffawed. "Did you hear that, boys? His secret weapon's a land squirrel!"

The pirates all shouted with laughter, but their laughter quickly died down when they heard someone whistling.

It was Sandy. She stood on the deck of Mr. Krabs's ship, leaning against a statue of a pirate carved out of solid rock. She kept whistling calmly for a moment, then stopped and grinned at the pirates on the other ship.

"HAI-YAA!" Sandy yelled as she leaped into the air and hit the top of the statue with a single karate chop. For a second, nothing happened. Then the statue crumbled into a million tiny pieces!

Crumbeard turned pale, and gulped. "You've got yourself a trade," he said to Mr. Krabs.

# chapter eight

Mr. Krabs was sailing the Krusty Krab back to Bikini Bottom with SpongeBob, Patrick, Squidward, and Sandy. The pirates had sailed off in the opposite direction on the yellow ship with the red trim, after they lowered the flag with the red crab and raised their Jolly Roger.

"Thanks for rescuing us, Mr. Krabs," said SpongeBob gratefully.

"Don't mention it, boy," Mr. Krabs said with a little smile. "I couldn't let 'em take my restaurant, could I? Especially after you made it look so good!"

"And thank you, Sandy!" SpongeBob said to his friend.

"Aw, shucks, SpongeBob," she answered. "That was nothin'. I'm just happy to bring y'all back to Bikini Bottom!"

SpongeBob glanced over at Squidward, who was lying on a deck chair sunbathing. Then he turned back to Mr. Krabs. "So how was it, sailing a ship again, seeing new places, meeting new people?"

Mr. Krabs thought for a moment. "To tell you the truth, SpongeBob, it was a little exhausting."

"Then you're not giving up the restaurant business?" SpongeBob asked hopefully.

"Give it up?" cried Mr. Krabs. "Of course not! How could I ever stop selling the famous sandwich I named after myself?"

SpongeBob smiled. "Oh, so *that's* why they're called Krabby Patties!" He looked up at the crow's nest. "Did you hear that, Patrick?"

But all Patrick said was, "BIKINI BOTTOM, HO!"

They were finally home, happy to be land-lubbers again.